Thanks for all of your support

Elizate

Callie

ELLIE LANTOS

Copyright © 2017 by Ellie Lantos.

All rights reserved. No part of this publication may be reproduced, distributed, or transmitted in any form or by any means, including photocopying, recording, or other electronic or mechanical methods, without the prior written permission of the publisher, except in the case of brief quotations embodied in critical reviews and certain other noncommercial uses permitted by copyright law. For permission requests, write to the publisher, addressed "Attention: Permissions Coordinator," at the address below.

BookVenture Publishing LLC
1000 Country Lane Ste 300
Ishpeming MI 49849
www.bookventure.com
Hotline: 1(877) 276-9751
Fax: 1(877) 864-1686

Ordering Information:
Quantity sales. Special discounts are available on quantity purchases by corporations, associations, and others. For details, contact the publisher at the address above.

Printed in the United States of America.

ISBN-13:	Softcover	978-1-64166-035-8
	Pdf	978-1-64166-036-5
	ePub	978-1-64166-037-2
	Kindle	978-1-64166-038-9

Rev. date: 10/04/2017

The last time I saw her, she drove off in her car. I don't know where she went or if she is coming back or if she is even alive but I know that I miss her. My Callie, my only, my mom. She decided one day that she couldn't take it anymore, couldn't take living in a house that was a constant fight for her. So she got in her car and left. She had given up.

I wrote in my journal on the five-year anniversary of my mom leaving my family. I was sad, so much stuff had happened because of her leaving. I needed to talk to someone to get my mind off of her. So I called Spring, my best friend, so that we could talk about the weekend ahead of us. We were planning on going to the mall and just walking around.

I had picked up the phone and was about to call her when I heard a knock at the door, me being the only one home at the time I had to get it. When I opened it I saw a familiar face—my mom.

"What are you doing here?" I asked her trying to be calm.

"I needed to come back," she replied slowly.

"Why are you here Callie?" I knew that calling her by her name was going to kill her but I didn't feel like she was my mom anymore. She looked different and you can't just leave someone for five years and expect to come back and have a warm welcome.

She flinched. "I told you, I needed to come back. I was missing you and your sister too much and I was lonely. I know that you probably hate me but can I please come in and talk to your father?" she asked, sounding tired.

"No you can't, do you know why? Because Dad left three years ago when he realized that you probably weren't going to ever come back. He told us that he was going out to try to find you. Then Ash and I got a call saying that the police had found his body below a bridge. He had gone off saying to Ash and I that he was going to try and find you when he was actually going to kill himself," I said, feeling the anger boil up.

She stood there looking shocked. "I thought that he hated me!" she said at last.

"No!" I said. "He really loved you and when you left it hurt all of us but it hurt him the most. He spent six months in your room not eating or sleeping just crying, and now he is dead," I told her.

"What about you and Ashley? How have you gotten along?" she asked.

"We almost got put in a girl's home but the police gave me a chance to take care of the both of us and it has worked out so far. I dropped out of school and work two jobs to pay for Ash's school and the house and everything." I started to tear up after I said that only because I was getting to a part that I don't like to talk about. "Now I can't pay for anything because I got fired from one of my jobs and can't find another, Ash is sick and in the hospital. I can't even pay for that! I have been borrowing from Spring and her family. The little she has left to give at least." I knew that after I said that I was going to be in tears, and I was.

"Oh my gosh, Alice! Why didn't you call me? Why didn't you let them put you in a girl's home?" she said, sounding sorry for us.

"I didn't call you because I didn't know where you were or if you had your cell phone or if you ever wanted to talk to your own daughter, you just left us. I didn't let them put us in a girl's home because I knew that we would be put in foster homes possibly separated and I couldn't do that to Ash. Not after her mother left and then her dad killed himself. She couldn't handle anymore anyways."

"I am so sorry that I left. I didn't know that it would have this effect on the family. If you will allow me I would like to see Ashley and the home." She seemed actually sorry, but I didn't know about what I would let her do. Not after everything she had done to us.

"I don't know about you seeing Ash but I will let you into the house only because I am tired of standing out here. Maybe if you can prove to me that you are actually going to stay and take care of us, then I will let you see Ash" I said. With me still being mad at her she will have to prove that she can see and take care of Ash in her condition.

When Callie got into the house she seemed happy. I guess she was happy to be home, even though this wasn't really her home. I knew that I should tell her why Ash was in the hospital at some point, but I wanted her to ask me.

As if she heard my thoughts, she asked, "You said that Ashley is in the hospital, why?"

I took a deep breath and told her, "Well, when Dad died she went into depression and wanted to drop out of school like me. I told her no because she needed an education more than I did. So she decided that she would get herself kicked out of school so that I would have no choice but to take care of her. She started getting into fights and ended up getting really hurt in some of them. One day, she got in a fight with a really big, tough kid and didn't win, she got knocked out and had broken bones. When the ambulance came they told me that she was in shock from the loss of blood." At this point I was crying, but I had to finish what had happened. "When she came out of shock she didn't recognize me. The only thing that she remembered was you. That you had left and caused Dad's death."

"Oh my god! You are afraid of her seeing me and causing something that will do damage to her." She understood some of why I won't let her see Ash.

"Well, that and you caused all of this, this whole domino effect on my family. You caused Dad to die and me to drop out, then leading to Ash wanting to drop out, me saying no, and her almost getting herself killed. I am mad at you. I thought that if you did show up I would be happy, but no! I am mad because you ruined our lives."

"I didn't mean for all of this to happen to this family. I just needed some time to myself." Callie didn't want to accept what she had done.

"Five years of alone time? Maybe if you had just told us that you were going to come back and just needed to be alone for a little bit none of this would have happened!" I said yelling but trying to calm myself. "I need to call someone, if you will just wait here." I said sharply, leaving the room. I immediately went up to call Spring.

"Hey, honey," she answered her phone.

"Hey. I need to tell you something . . ." I started.

"Ok, what is it?" she asked, sounding worried.

"Well, Callie is back. She showed up at our house today wanting to come in, now she wants to see Ash and I don't know if I trust her completely. What do I do?" I asked fairly quickly.

"What a minute, you mean your mom, Callie?" her baffled reply came.

"Yes," I simply told her.

"I say don't let her see Ash. She left you and caused a dramatic time period. I just don't want you to get hurt even more." This is why Spring was my best friend, she knew exactly what I needed from her.

"She knows," I said, starting to regret what I had told Callie. "I told her about Dad and why Ash is in the hospital. She seems actually sorry for what she did. She is in the living room right now, do you think that you could come over and be my shoulder to lean on?" I asked sweetly.

"Oh my gosh! You didn't even have to ask! I will be there in promptly two point two seconds." Then she hung up. Knowing that she was coming, and was going to help me, gave me the courage to go back to the living room to talk to Callie.

When I got back to the couch she was looking through an old photo album. I didn't want her to know that I was there so I scurried to the kitchen that was connected to the living room. While I was watching her I noticed tears running down her cheeks and she would periodically run her hand over a picture. She reminded me so much of Ash and I wanted to be glad that she was back. The thing that stopped me was all that she had caused my sister and I to go through.

In the middle of me snooping I heard the front door open and Spring call, "Babe, I'm here."

"In the kitchen!" I yelled back. She came to the kitchen and I turned back to watch Callie. She didn't seem to have stopped looking at the pictures to see who was here.

"Has she been looking at those the whole time?" Spring asked. She seemed even more baffled now that she was here and could see Callie.

"I don't know, I came here after I called you and she was doing that. Can you talk to her please, I don't know what to do." I was desperate for her to do something.

"Sure," Spring said as she left the kitchen.

I watched as she went up to Callie. When she started to talk I couldn't hear what she was saying, I could only watch what Callie's reaction was. After a little bit Spring started heading back towards me, toward the kitchen.

"How did it go? What did you say?" I asked.

"It went fine, I said that you were really hurt and not sure what to do. I told her that you have been dealing with the loss of both of your parents and almost your little sister and that you were mad at her for not contacting them. She said that she understood what you have been through, and I said that she really didn't because her mom didn't walk out on her causing her dad to kill himself. She doesn't understand the feeling of having your little sibling in the hospital with nothing you could do for them. She didn't say anything after that except that she wanted to talk with you. I came back here to get you and now I am here," Spring explained what happened.

"I don't know if I can talk to her without getting mad at her. I mean, I can try but I would like you to be there with me." I was so glad that Spring cared for me the way she did.

"All right, let's go." And we left the kitchen.

When we got to the couch where Callie was sitting I took a deep breath and Spring gave me a reassuring look. I sat down across from the couch, in a chair and waited for her to say something.

"Could I talk to you alone?" she asked, finally speaking up, eyeing Spring.

"No, whatever you want to say to me you can say in front of the both of us," I answered, not wanting Spring to leave.

"First thing that I want to ask you is . . . are you two dating?"

I was shocked that that was the first thing that she wanted to know out of everything. "No, we are not dating. She is my best friend," I answered, showing the shock in my voice.

"It just seemed like it because when she walked in she called you 'Babe' and you both seem very protective of each other," she said.

"No. Like I told you, her family is the ones who have been supporting Ash and I. She has been paying for the hospital bills, paying for the house. They are the ones who have become my family." As I was talking I felt Spring's hand on my shoulder. "That is why she is so protective of me, because I am her 'sister' and she doesn't want anything bad to happen to me." I knew that Spring was proud of me but could see the look of disappointment on her face. I knew that she wanted me to tell the truth but I didn't know if I could do it in that moment.

"Ok, I was just wondering. My second question is, is there any way that I can prove to you that I can be a good mom again so that you can let me see Ashley?" Callie asked.

Spring answered for me, "I don't think so."

I gave her a look that said, I can do this myself, and replied, "I don't know. You left us and I don't know if I will ever be able to trust you. I don't know what Ash would do if I let you see her and I can't put her in that situation." I wanted her to know that I didn't trust her and that I might not.

"I understand that you care for your sister and I love that, I just still can't get over the fact that you two look so much like you are dating. I don't want to pry so I will leave it alone. I just want you to think about it." She still wanted to know if Spring and I were dating! I was so surprised. She just learned that her family had fallen apart because of her leaving and that is what she was stuck on.

"Let me talk with Spring and I will be back." I said, getting up, dragging Spring to my room.

When I shut the door Spring immediately asked, "Why didn't you tell her that we are dating? Are you not proud of us?"

"Of course I am proud of us, I just don't trust her yet and when the time comes then I will tell her. On the other hand, what should I do about her wanting to gain my trust again?" I asked.

"Even though I am just as mad at her as you are, I think that you should give her a chance and if she does anything that you don't like keep it in mind when she asks to see Ash again. Tell her some rules to abide by and that if she keeps doing things that you don't like she won't be able to see Ash," Spring said. "I also think that you should tell her about us because then it lets her know how you live and what she should avoid saying to you about certain things."

"I guess that I will try that. I will tell her about us and that I do have some rules that she has to follow. Let's go back downstairs" I said, repeating what Spring had said to me to get it in my brain. I had decided that I would try to trust her instead of shutting her out completely. As we started to go back downstairs I started to think about some rules for her to follow and about Ash and how I was going to tell her about our mom coming back after five years and about Spring and how much I loved her and how much she loved me.

"Callie, I have a couple of things to tell you. The first thing is that I lied to you about Spring and I not dating, we actually are."

She interrupted, "Thank you so much!" She seemed happy just to know that we were dating, I didn't understand it.

"The second thing is that I am willing to give you a chance to gain back my trust. But I do have some rules that I will need you to follow in order to do so."

She interrupted again, "I will do anything." I could see the desperation in her eyes.

I continued, "The first thing is that you accept me and Spring into your life because I live here and Spring is my girlfriend and basically does too. The second thing is that you don't pry, don't become so desperate that you are digging into everything that I do. Third, is that you respect my decision on everything, I have become the mom here and I don't need anything to mess up my family again. Fourth, is that you don't ask about Ash because I really don't like talking about her and I will let you see her when I feel that I can trust you." I felt really confident saying that and I felt that she was going to try and follow those rules only because she seemed to really want to be a part of our lives.

She answered back immediately, "That seems fair. I will do my best to follow those rules and earn your trust I really do want to be able to be in your lives again."

"Thank you, now I just want to spend time with Spring." With that, Spring and I left to go up to my room. I know that I should have been maybe a little more tough with Callie or maybe had a few more rules for her to follow but I didn't have the energy anymore to talk to her and argue, and I felt like she was actually going to try.

When I had closed the door to my room Spring just stared at me. "What?" I asked not knowing why she was staring at me.

"I am just very proud to have you as my girlfriend. I think that you handled that very well and I just love you." She looked at me like I was her only hope but I don't know what for.

"Thank you for being here for me. I am very happy to have you as my girlfriend and I love you too." I really did love her and was so glad she supported me.

"Yay!" she said, still with that glimmer of hope in her eyes.

"You are looking at me like I am your only hope, what are you having trouble with that you haven't told me about? You know you can tell me anything." I wanted to know what was bothering her.

"I just really love you and nothing big is bothering me at the moment." I could tell Spring was avoiding telling me.

"I still know that there is something bothering you and I want to know and be there for you like you were here for me today, please tell me." I knew something was wrong but I didn't know what. She got along with her family, she had good grades in school, she had an almost perfect world, I don't know what she could have been upset about.

"I am a little off because of my brother. It looks like he decided to run off, kind of like Callie did. Nobody knows why or where, we just know that he is gone. We have told the police that he is missing. He didn't even leave a note saying where he was going or anything, and you know the situation is kind of like yours and I just don't know what to do." At this point she started to cry, "I have had feelings of him standing behind me and saying that it is too late for him to come back. I feel like he has been kidnapped. On top of all of this, I am trying to deal with it without showing it to my sister, she is the one who told me that he was gone." She barely finished that sentence because she was crying so hard.

"Oh my gosh! Why didn't you tell me earlier?" I was conflicted between wanting to hold her and wanting to smack her at the same time. I wanted to help her but I didn't know how.

"I didn't tell you because I was still trying to deal with it myself and I didn't think that telling you would help me because I thought you would freak out. Then you called me over because of Callie and I didn't want to stress you out with anything of my problems." I could tell she was trying to hold back her feelings which she almost never did that around me.

"Well, I am not freaking out. I just wish that you had told me earlier so that I could have helped you. I can tell that you are struggling with this and I hope that you will be able to tell me everything when you are ready." I was freaking out but I didn't want to show her that. I was going to let her go slow with what she told me but I still really wanted to know what she was going through and feeling just didn't want to push it.

"Thank you for understanding that I need a little time to process it myself. I will definitely tell you when I have figured out how to deal with him leaving. I don't actually know why he left and I don't like it. I haven't gotten any sleep the past couple of nights because I keep thinking that he left because of something that I did or that he didn't like how the family treated him, because, you know, he was kind of the underdog." She was becoming broken down. She couldn't keep her feelings in anymore and was pouring them out, she does that. "Hunter always seemed like he was a happy-go-lucky kid and that nothing ever bothered him, but I guess that it did and he just kept it all inside and couldn't deal with it anymore. I just can't believe that he left, I guess I wished he would have talked to me rather than doing what he did. I just miss him so much." Spring ended up in tears again lying in my bed with her head on my lap. She was sobbing and couldn't speak very clearly anymore, she kept going on but I couldn't understand her.

As I took in the information that she just told me, I started thinking about what could have caused her little brother to run away. I just hated seeing her like this and I knew that the only way to make her feel better is to help her find her brother or why he left so that she can have some closure. It reminds me of how I felt when Callie left—helpless.

"Look," I said, trying to be calm and nice. "I think that you just need some relaxing time to yourself, so why don't you go and get a massage. I can handle Callie on my own now and you deserve it." I knew that she just needed to try and forget about her brother for just a little bit so that she could relax.

"Thank you so much! I will definitely call you with updates as I get them." She left to go relax and I walked down to talk to Callie.

She was still sitting on the couch looking at the picture books. I didn't know whether to be mad that she was going through my life or to let her so that she could see what she had missed out on.

"Callie," I said, breaking her concentration. "I am sure that you have a bunch of questions." I had really hoped that she didn't, but I knew that she did.

"Actually," she started. "I was just looking through some of your pictures and I was wondering where they were taken." Of course she would want to know that.

"Those were family pictures that we took right before Dad died. I knew that something was up with him so I decided to get pictures taken with him before anything happened." I explained all of this while trying to remain calm.

She looked at me like I was a wounded puppy, I hated it. But I knew that if I could trust her I would have to put the things that I hated about her aside. "I saw your father in some of them but a couple are just you and Ashley. You look very sad. Was that after your dad died?" Callie was straight on point. I noticed that she hadn't called Dad, dad. She said your dad, as if she didn't even want to be associated with him.

"Yes. We had just been told that we might be separated so we decided to get pictures together to have to remember each other." I knew that if she kept asking questions I would start crying again. So I asked her to not ask anymore.

Most people would be delighted to have their mom come back after five years. But after what she caused my family to go through made me want to hate her, but I didn't for some reason. She is still my mom and now that she is back and wanting to know what is going on and happened in my life makes me want to love her. I knew that in the back of my mind, there was still the slither of hatred toward her.

"I know that me coming back is hard for you, but I am so glad that you are giving me a second chance to come back into the family. I promise that I will respect your wishes and your space," Callie said. "Could I sleep here or should I find a hotel or somewhere else to sleep?" she asked.

"I don't know yet," I answered. "I think that it would be best for you to get a hotel or a different place in the beginning and just come over, just so that we can get used to having each other around. I have gotten used to being the head of the house and would appreciate it if I could have some space when you are here. I also need time to decide if I am going to let you sleep here at all and that will just take trusting you and getting to know that you won't do anything that will harm me or Ash." I finished honestly. "And I know that you want to be a part of this family again, I just don't know how to let that happen." I added after thinking for a while.

"I will find a hotel nearby so that if you need me you can just call me. I also want to thank you again for giving me this second chance." After giving me a phone number, she left.

After Callie left I decided to call Spring so I could go get a massage with her. She told me that she hadn't ended up going to the massage and that made me worried. She told me that she had sat in her room for the hour and just couldn't bring herself to leave.

"I tried to get up after I had gotten my shoes on and I did, but then I passed my brother's room and everything that I was worried about came flooding in and I had to come running back in here because I was crying. I didn't want to call you because I need to sort this out myself but I think that it would have been better if I had you by my side for comfort. I just feel like everything is spiraling out of hand with both of our families," she explained.

"Spring, babe, I know that this is hard for you to go through, but you just need to go and get relaxed and stop thinking about it for a little bit. I am going to take you to get a massage and we will go together. It'll be a date." I wanted her to relax and not worry about anything for a while. She needed to be able to not think and I think that doing this will let me think about what I am going to do about Callie.

"Okay," she said kind of sadly. "I will go with you but I am not promising to stop thinking about it for forever."

"I know that won't be possible, I just need you to relax for a little bit and not think about anything because it is making you worked up. When you get worked up you tend to shut down. That isn't good for you. It doesn't help your situation," I said worryingly.

"I know. I am trying not to get worked up but sometimes it just can't happen. I just end up like this and I can't control it." Spring was really worked up, I could tell she was starting to break down and I needed her to calm down.

"Sit down," I told her. "You will feel better if you sit down and just be quiet for a little bit." So she did. I could tell that she felt instantly better. It's like she needed to find her internal balance and just having something solid to sit on helped.

"You need to go back to deal with Callie," she said. "I am sure that she is doing something to snoop around or even trying to see Ash."

"You have just moved your worrying from your brother to me. I think that she is very trustworthy because she really wants to impress me. But I will leave you alone so that you can relax and think about everything and nothing." I left her so that she can just be alone and talk with herself about what she is going to do. I needed to go and be by myself and think about how I was going to deal with Callie if she did anything that broke the rules. I wanted to go see Ash but I didn't know if I would be able to hold back that our mother was back. If I did tell her I didn't know how she was going to react because of her injuries. But, I decided that she would find out eventually, better off now and from me.

So, I headed to the hospital and went to Ash's room. When I walked in she was asleep and I didn't want to disturb her so I sat next to her bed. She woke up a couple minutes after I came in.

"Who are you?" she asked.

It broke my heart every time she asked, "I am your sister, remember?"

"Oh, yeah. You took care of me before I came here." She still looked confused.

"Well, you didn't come here by choice. You got in a fight and lost a lot of blood. Do you remember that?" I had to be timid because it could jog her memory too much and she could lunge at me. It did happen once, it was terrifying.

"Yeah, I remember that. I also know that Dad died and Mom left."

"Actually, that is what I am here to talk to you about." I started out slowly because I didn't know how she would react. "I have run into someone and she is a family friend and is very nice and wants to help us and get to know us."

"Well, who is it?" she asked, returning back to her original self.

"I ran into, Mom." I said quietly.

She sat there looking like she is processing information.

"What?" she asked very softly.

"She showed up at the doorstep this morning and wants to get to know us. She said that she didn't want to hurt us or anything." I wanted her to believe that Callie didn't want to hurt us and wanted the best for the both of us.

"How do you know if she is telling the truth?" she asked.

"That is the thing, I don't. She wants to come see you and talk to you, would it be okay if she came over?" I didn't want to push anything on her too fast.

"I mean, I guess so. I will try to not freak out on her." Smiling at her, I knew that she meant it.

"If you are okay with it I will bring her by tomorrow. I don't want it to be tonight." I didn't want her to have too much on her plate tonight.

"I think that would be fine." She sounded very confident.

"All right, I will tell her. For now, you need some rest." I left her to herself so that she can sleep.

As I drove home I thought about what Callie had said and what Ash had said. I am glad that Ash wanted to see Callie, then Callie could see what she put us through. Callie would be able to see the effects of leaving a family for five years and causing a death and how that leaves the family.

When I got home Callie was asleep on the couch. I knew that she would wake up soon. So I would tell her when she woke up. I went to my room and called Spring to see how she was getting along. She didn't answer which made me worried because she almost always answered her phone.

So I left her a message, "Hey, babe. I was just calling to see how you're doing. If you need anything just call. Love you." I needed her to call me back so that I could talk to her.

"Hey, Spring, just calling again to check on you. Making sure you are okay. Don't forget about our date!" Spring did it again, she didn't answer her phone, that's two days now. And we have a date. She loved our dates even if they are stupid. I was going to give her time because she was going through a tough time in her life like me and I didn't want to bother her.

Around 3:30 in the afternoon Spring called me back saying that she was sorry that she missed my call and that she was at the police station with her sister to help with the investigation of her brother. I told her it was fine and that I had figured that she was probably doing something important.

"Alice, I am ready to go see Ashley at the hospital." I heard Callie say from downstairs.

"Okay," I replied. "Just let me call ahead so that they know that you are coming." Because of what had happened to Ash the hospital staff knew what had happened to our family, so they would be protective of Ash and make sure she wasn't pushed too far.

Then, we were on our way. As I was driving, I was wondering what exactly was going to happen and why Callie was so interested in seeing Ash other than the fact that she, too, was her daughter. So I asked, "Why are you so interested in Ash and going to visit her? I know that she is your daughter but these past years I have been her mom and her dad. She trusts me, and I am pretty sure that that is the only reason she's okay with you coming to visit her."

Callie sighed and thought for a while, eyes looking out her window. "Well, I have missed a huge chunk of your girls' lives and I want to get caught up. I want to thank you for telling me what happened to Ashley and why she is in the state that she is in. I want to see her and hopefully be able to comfort her."

"You can't touch her," I interrupted.

"Why not? Did I do something to retract my privilege?" she asked.

"No, I can't even touch her. She freaks out with me because she thinks that she is going to get attacked again. I don't want anything to happen to her. And part of that is why I called ahead, because the hospital staff knows what caused Ash to be in the hospital and they are going to be on guard with you around," I explained.

She didn't like that at all. "Are they like that with you?"

I could tell that she was hurt that I called ahead and that she won't get the peaceful visit she was hoping for. "No, but I have been there every day for the past year. Ash might not recognize me when I first get there every time but she figures it out and knows that I am not there to hurt her."

"Oh, okay. I won't do anything, I promise," Callie said.

And with that we were at the hospital. I led Callie to Ash's room and offered that I go in first so that she saw me before anyone else. When I walked in I saw Ash's favorite nurse sitting next to the bed just talking to Ash. I smiled, knowing that she was only there for support. "Hi," I said and walked in. Ash looked over at me with a confused look and then she recognized me.

"Hi, sister!" she said with such joy.

"Remember the person I came and talked to you about yesterday?"

I ask her. "Well, she wanted to visit you today. So I brought her with me this time."

"Oh, okay." I could tell that Ash tensed up. I leaned out and told Callie that it was okay just to stay standing and to just walk through the door, not toward Ash.

As Callie walked through the door I could see her holding her breath, this was the first time that she was seeing her youngest daughter after abandoning her when she was three.

"Hi," she said tentatively. "How are you?"

I looked at her cautiously, trying to tell her not to push too much. I was also watching Ash to make sure that she was okay with what was happening.

"I'm okay, who are you again?" Ash asked. I could see the look of sadness on Callie's face because of her own daughter not recognizing her, and that she couldn't tell the truth about who she was.

"She is just someone who wants to see you and make sure that you are doing okay. Remember, I told you about bringing her to see you." I explained for her. Ash looked like she wasn't completely on board with this whole new visitor thing. "We can come back tomorrow if you want, we don't have to stay," I said, hoping to make her feel better.

"No, you can stay," Ash said. I always forget that her vocabulary has dwindled since she has been here because of the damage to her brain. The doctors say that it is a miracle that she can still talk.

"Okay." Callie and I say at the same time. So, we sat and I talked to Ash about what was happening in my life, with Spring and her brother, and everything because I knew that she wasn't going to tell anyone. As I was telling her, I noticed that she was staring at Callie. "Do you want to say something to her?" I asked Callie. "She seems to be interested in you, maybe she has some questions."

"Oh, yeah. I was just watching you twos relationship because it is so special. Do you have any questions, Ashley?" Callie said softly.

"Well, I guess I was just seeing what you looked like. Because you don't look anything like I remember, but I was also very little when you left so I don't remember a lot. Then I was wondering why you left because I haven't been able to find a reason throughout these years. And then, I was wondering if you had known what had happened to Dad and if you had thought about coming back to take care of us, and that led me back to my first question, why did you leave us? Is there really a good explanation?" Ash let out all of her thoughts. I was expecting this because when she gets into deep thought and you interrupt, she just finishes thinking out loud.

"Wow, that is a lot of thinking," Callie said. "I guess that there really isn't a good reason why I left. I didn't feel like I belonged with your father and that I didn't belong in this town. So I left."

"But you left me and Alice and Dad and then Dad went and killed himself. How could you do that?" Ash asked, getting worked up.

"I guess I don't really have a good reason. I thought you girls were going to be okay," Callie said, trying to keep her voice calm.

"But why. I don't know why you wouldn't have told anyone because so many terrible things happened after you left. I mean with Dad and then me and everything. The only way we are allowed to live by ourselves is because the sheriff knows who we are and because Alice and Spring are kind of in the same situation," Ash said. I saw her getting worked up and decided that she needed a breather.

"Hey, Callie, let me introduce you to the nurse who has been helping me with raising Ash and been at Ash's side whenever she needed anything." I was hoping this would work to get them separated.

"Okay, I'd like to thank her for all she has done to help you girls," Callie said. So, off we went to find the nurse. I led Callie to our normal meeting spot hoping that the nurse would be there. When she wasn't I went to the front desk area and found her filing some paperwork.

"Hey, Alison. There is someone I'd like you to meet," I said. "This is Callie, my mom." I added the last part quietly to try to not get anyone else involved, you don't want to see a hospital staff go off on a family, especially not this staff and Callie.

"Hi, Alison. I just wanted to thank you for all that you have done to help my girls," Callie said, she sounded like she was ending Alison's employment with us.

"Well, it's better than what you have done for them," Alison replied. She has always had some hard feelings for our mother because I have told her everything that has happened. "I mean, what kind of person leaves their two daughters alone? How does that make you any kind of a mother?" Alison exclaimed.

"Well, I guess I am not a very good one. I am trying to make up for it though," Callie tried saying.

"I don't know how possible that is for you. Do you know how many people in this hospital know what kind of pain you have caused these girls? Everybody does. I doubt you would be able to even be legally in charge of them without getting a fight from someone, maybe even everyone, in the community," Alison said.

"I didn't realize how important these girls were to you, guys. I am so thankful that they have had you to support them during these years," Callie said, surprised but still sounding like she was dismissing Alison.

"Yeah, Spring's family too. I don't know how much you know about them but the entire town has helped raise these two families and if anyone tries to hurt them, they will have to deal with our entire population," Alison said.

"Good to know. I am not here to hurt them, or anyone. I hope people can understand that. I also hope that people can realize that Alice isn't going to let me off the hook anytime soon," Callie said.

"I know that, I think we all do. I just wanted to give you a fair warning about what you are up against," said Alison.

Alison was the best that we could ever ask for. She took care of me and Ash, as well as Spring and her siblings even when we didn't need it. I don't know what we would have done without her. Alison was my mom more than Callie was and sometimes I mistakenly called her Mom.

"Thanks, Mom, oh sorry. Thanks, Alison," I said, correcting myself, smirking on the inside.

"No problem, Alice, I hope everything works out for you guys," Alison said.

I could tell that me calling Alison Mom hurt Callie because she was supposed to be my mom but I really didn't care. She hadn't earned that title and Alison had truly been like a mom to Ash and me.

"So, I guess we will go back and say goodbye to Ash and then we can go home. I need to check on Spring," I said to Callie. We made our way back to her room and I noticed that her light was off, so I assumed she was sleeping so we didn't go in.

As we went home I called Spring again to make sure that she was okay, and again there was no answer. I was continuing to get worried.

"Hello again, I was just checking on you to make sure you were okay. I hope that we can still go on that date tonight, we can always reschedule if you need to." I left her another message, number three.

When we were home I saw Spring sitting on our porch. I was hoping to get good news but I had a feeling that wasn't going to happen as she looked like she had really been crying.

"Hey, Al. I needed to get away for a little. I had to be so brave for my little sister and now it is all coming back to me that he might be gone forever and that it could have been my fault that he left in the first place and then I looked at her and saw that she was really freaked out. I don't know what to do." She got it all off her chest at once and then collapsed like it used up all of her energy.

"Wait a minute. Why do you think that your Hunter is your fault? There is no way that you could have caused any of this. If you need to stay with me you can, you know that. I have enough rooms for both you and your sister to come over, you know that. Don't worry about it. Everybody knows our situation and they will help us. I know it," I said, trying to give some confidence to her.

"I just think that if I would have paid more attention to him that he wouldn't have run away if that is what happened. If he even didn't run away, he could have gotten kidnapped and that makes me feel even worse. It is the same thing that could make him run away, I needed to pay more attention to him." The confidence I had tried to give hadn't worked.

"This is in no way your fault and I want you to know that. You have always paid attention to your brother and you love him, he knows that, doing this couldn't have been because of you," I said. I noticed Callie kind of hanging back and I was glad that she was not butting into our conversation, but I could also tell that she was listening to what we were saying. I looked back at her and motioned for her to come inside for some dinner, with Spring as well.

We went inside and ate in silence. "I guess I should go home and check on my sister," Spring said.

"I think I should go too. I have to get back before they close the front doors at the hotel," Callie said. It was weird to me that Callie said that, I didn't think that they locked the doors of hotels because of the late night people. They both left, leaving me in my thoughts about what to do with everything that has happened these past couple of days.

I went to clean the kitchen with some music on. I needed something to distract my mind for a little bit. As I was cleaning I heard a little scuffling behind me and turned to find what looked like Hunter, Spring's brother. In my mind I was freaking out, I didn't know what to do, so I walked forward trying not to scare him. He walked back, not wanting to get too close to me, so I stopped, still freaking out. I turned back to cleaning the dishes and putting them away, my mind racing, and heard him again, it sounded like he was walking toward me. But when I looked back again, he wasn't there. I didn't know what to do, with Callie being here and then him going missing from his own house, this was really freaking me out. I thought it would be good to call Spring and let her know what happened.

"Hey," she answered.

"Hey, what's up?" I replied trying to calm my voice but I could hear my nerves seeping through.

"Nothing, just acting like everything's normal. I am making dessert for Molly and I and about to sit down and watch a movie. What about you?"

"Well, I am actually calling because I saw Hunter in my kitchen," I said, trying not to yell at her.

"What? What do you mean?" She sounded tense, she was trying not to yell and disturb Molly.

"When I was cleaning up the dishes I thought I heard something behind me, so I turned around and he was just standing there. When I tried to walk forward he just walked back, it seemed like he didn't want to get close to me. I didn't know what to do so I turned around and continued to work to see if he would come back. And then I thought I heard him walk toward my back again but when I turned around he wasn't there," I explained, trying to keep my voice calm.

"That is crazy! That is what I was telling you about when I said that

I kept having a feeling like it was too late to save him or something! I keep seeing him whenever I turn around and he just stands there. What the heck do we do? I mean, why is he doing this, where is he? I need help, I don't know how to handle this," she said, sobbing.

"Well, even though I never doubted you, now I really believe you. It's freaking me out," I said. "I am going to start thinking of a plan, I think we need to start with the police. Anyway, I will let you get back to your movie, talk to you later." And with that, I hung up. When I turned around, Hunter was there again, but he seemed to be more present.

"Hi, Hunter," I said. "How are you?" I didn't know what I was expecting him to say, but when he didn't say anything, I was a little disappointed. "I just wanted to let you know that Spring is really worried about you and really misses you." Still trying to be calm and not scare him away.

He just stood there, like he was studying me. Then I felt it, it was the strangest feeling I've ever felt, this boy in front of me was cold, I could feel the energy coming off him. Panicked, I reached out quickly to touch him and before my hand came near his face he was gone. Why was all of this happening to me and my family?

Instead of calling Spring again I figured that I would just go to bed and try to sleep it off, so I went upstairs to my room and settled into my soft blankets and drifted into the relaxed darkness of the night.

"Callie, what are you doing here? It's the middle of the night."

"I don't know, I just wanted to see you." Callie seemed weird, her eyes were glazed over and she wasn't talking normally.

"Well, you should just go back to the hotel because I don't really want to see you right now." I didn't want to sound harsh but it happened to come out that way. *"Are you okay, you don't seem right. Not that I know what*

that is because you have been missing out of my life for the past five years," I said, adding the last part to hurt her.

"I know that. I just want to make it up to you," she said.

"And how exactly are you going to do that?" I asked.

"Well, I think I have an idea of where your girlfriend's brother is," she said hesitantly.

"What do you mean?" I asked suspiciously. I didn't want to trust her enough to give me that information.

"You know how Spring had been saying that she felt like she had been seeing him in her house or felt like it was too late for her to get him back? Well, I might have had something to do with it," she said, backing up a little.

"What!" I yelled. "How could you have done that to her. And then for you to meet her and hear what is happening to her and not say anything about it! That is just insane and there is now a way bigger chance of you not getting my trust back."

"I know, I know. I was just trying to come here so I asked him and when he knew I asked if he would get in the car with me. He was outside of his house getting the mail and it seemed like it was okay to ask him," she tried to explain.

"Okay, I can understand the asking, but why did you want him in your car? That is just weird!" I said.

"I wasn't in my right mind and I needed someone to talk to. He was just there. When he actually got in I didn't know what to do because I have never been in this situation . . ."

I woke up the next morning in a cold sweat. My dream had made me thrash around in my sleep and I was all tangled up in my sheets, very hot. I didn't know what to do with what had just happened and normally I would call Spring, but I didn't want her to worry about anything more right now. So I went to visit Ash in the hospital, hoping that would get my mind off things for now.

When I got there Alison was taking out Ash's breakfast, only halfway eaten. As I walked into the room I noticed that Ash was sitting away from the door, which was unusual, so I waited a little. When she didn't turn around, and I knew that she had heard me come in, I got a worried. So I went to find Alison again and ask what was up.

"Hey, everything okay with Ash? I noticed she didn't eat her breakfast," I asked.

"Yeah, we don't quite know yet, the last time we saw her like this she didn't eat for weeks. I don't know if you should bring Callie back, I have a suspicion that she might have something to do with this," she said.

"Okay, I can understand that." And with that I left, not wanting to disturb Ash anymore. As I was walking I found myself going to Spring's house, so I figure that I might as well talk to her. When I knocked on the door she didn't answer, there was no yelling that it would be a second or scrambling to get to the door in the middle of cleaning or playing or anything. So, I let myself in as I normally do anyway.

"Hello?" I called, still no answer. "You there, Spring? I need to talk to you," I said. I walked through the house, through her room and the kitchen. She wasn't there. So I went home, and again found her on my front porch.

"Hey, I went to your house looking for you. I have so much to tell you," I told her. She didn't look up or move at all, she just sat there staring at her hands.

"You okay, Spring?" I asked, stepping forward.

"I don't know, I think I am depressed. I can't think of anything not sad and I know that I can't do this to my sister but I don't know what to do," she said.

I had to think for a little, that wasn't what I had expected her to say.

"Well, why don't you come in? I will make some soup and we can talk, like I said, I have a lot to tell you."

When we went in and got the soup started I sat down and started to talk. "So, after I called you and I turned around Hunter was behind me. He was different though so I thought I would talk to him. He didn't say anything and it looked like he was studying me. And then, I went to bed to sleep it off and I had a weird dream. Callie had come to my house in the middle of the night and told me that she had been the one who took Hunter. I didn't know what to do so I went to see Ash but she didn't eat her breakfast so I didn't want to bother her. Alison told me not to bring Callie anymore because she thought that she had something to do with it." I finished and waited for her reaction.

"Oh wow!" she said. "That is not what I thought you were going to say." She seemed to be kind of okay with it.

"You are really calm for what I just told you, are you okay? You said you wanted to talk, what's your deal?" I asked her. I was hoping that she would have some good news to counter my kind of bad news.

"I think that you should talk to Callie about your dream because who knows, this could be one of those psychic dreams. I don't have any update on Hunter other than what you just told me and I think that I should tell the police that we have been 'seeing' him around," Spring said. She was handling this so much better than I thought she would. I mean her brother is missing and I had a dream that my mom who just came back in my life took him.

As we thought we just looked at each other and then in a split second Hunter showed up behind her. "Umm, Spring, not to worry you or anything but I think you should turn around," I said, not taking my eyes off him. But as soon as she turned around he was gone.

"What was there?" she asked and I think that by the look on my face she knew what had just happened. "Are you kidding me, why does he keep coming here? It's like he doesn't even want to be at home."

"I don't know. It's like he doesn't want to be seen by you. If he comes back and you're not here I will try to talk to him again to see what information I can get," I said, hoping to calm her nerves about what might be happening to him. "And I will talk to Callie to see if she has anything to do with it, if you want to be there you can, I know you think you can tell when someone is lying." That is how we met so many years ago, she thought that I had been lying about something I can't even remember now and then we became best friends. Then, as we got to know each other, we got together. Just worked itself out to be that way.

"I don't know, I haven't had to use that in a while, the kids have been so good lately. But I think I want to be there just so that I can hear her answer myself," she said.

"Okay, I will call you when she comes over and you can come back. I think you should check on your sister, or you can bring her here. I just don't want her to feel like she is alone in this whole situation," I said. Her sister, Molly, was the sweetest little girl and I knew that there was no way that she wasn't panicking a little inside. Right as I said that the doorbell rang, and it was Callie.

"Hey, we were just about to go get Molly, Spring's sister, and bring her over. We will be right back, don't mess with anything," I told her, and then we left.

When we got back Callie was sitting on the couch looking through our pictures again, but this time she found the one that had some pictures of her in it.

"Hi, Callie, we have some things we want to talk to you about," I said. Then I turned to Molly. "You can go upstairs, I have a new toy for you to play with!" I told her. I had always kept a playroom for her.

"Okay. Shoot," Callie said once Molly had gone to play.

"Well, I would like to start with saying that I went to see Ash this morning and she hadn't eaten her breakfast. Alison said that the last she started doing this it was weeks before she ate again, and that I shouldn't bring you back in case that is what triggered it."

"Oh, my gosh. I am so sorry if I did cause it to start again," she said.

"I know, we really don't know exactly what causes her to do this but she does sometimes. And the second thing is that I had a dream last night that you confessed to me that you had taken Hunter," I said, waiting for her reaction. She didn't seem to have the kind of reaction that would lead me to think one way or another. I was hoping she would have made it a little easier to read her face.

"Well, it seems fair that you would think that but I don't know why you would trust a dream," she said, it sounded like she was trying to defend herself.

"So are you saying that you did take him? Because that is what it sounds like to me," I said.

"No, I am saying that it seems weird for you to trust a dream. I mean, they are just random things that your brain makes up. It just doesn't seem like something you would do." She started to get a little testy. "You don't even know what I would or wouldn't do. You don't even know me, who are you to judge me?"

I said, "I want a clear answer, did you or did you not take Hunter?" I pretty much yelled this at her without yelling, I didn't want Molly to come down and ask what was happening.

"Sweetie," she said.

"Don't call me that," I interrupted her.

"Okay, Alice, I don't know what happened to Hunter," she said, then she turned to Spring. "And I am sorry about your brother and that I don't have a way to help you," she finished.

Spring and I looked at each other and mentally both decided to go to my room and talk. "I think she is lying, she didn't give a firm yes or no. And I don't know which I would rather have," I said to Spring.

"I know what you mean, if she had said yes we could have someone to blame, and if she had said no then we could eliminate someone from the list. I think that we should give her time and ask her again," she said. I agreed and we went to go find Molly and make sure nothing was wrong.

When we got downstairs Callie was gone. It looked like she had gone through the photo book again but had left in a hurry, she had also eaten something, like a sandwich.

"Spring, I don't think she wants us to ask her again," I said staring at the mess that Callie had left.

"I think you're right, Alice. I think we need to tell the police and go check on Ash to make sure she is okay," she said. Spring always knew what to do in these kinds of situations.

So we left and went to the police station. When we got there everyone greeted us and asked how the rest of our family were doing and they asked Spring if she had heard anything about Hunter.

"Well, that is what I came here to talk to you guys about." She started for me. They led us to a room so that we could talk to someone.

"What's up, guys, I am hoping you have a lead on Hunter," the officer said.

"Actually, you know Callie, Alice and Ash's mom?" Spring said.

"Yeah."

"She has come back. She came back a couple of days ago," Spring told him.

"What? Why didn't you come and tell us?" he said to me.

"I don't know. I was all freaked out that she knew where we lived still and that she actually want to be a part of my life, our life. I didn't know what to do," I said.

"You should have, we could have protected you from her," he said.

"I don't think she wants to hurt us, except for why we are here . . ." I said, but I couldn't finish the sentence.

"We think that Callie had something to do with Hunter," Spring said for me.

"What makes you think that?" the officer asked us. We told him our story about how she had answered and how she had left in what looked like a hurry. "Can I come see your house or have you cleaned up already?" he asked.

"I haven't cleaned up anything and you can go. We are just going to check on Ash to make sure she is okay," I told him.

"That's fine. We will go while you are there, see you soon." And with that, we parted. Spring and I to the hospital and a couple of officers to my house.

When we got to the hospital, Ash was awake, at least for the time being. She seemed to be doing okay, she had a small stack of crackers because she hadn't eaten her breakfast.

"Hey, how are you doing?" I asked her and I was met with the look of a girl who had just been traumatized.

"I . . . I am o . . . okay," she stuttered out. But she didn't seem to be okay.

"Okay, I just wanted to tell you that Callie isn't going to come here anymore and that she can't hurt you," I said to her, I didn't want to get into all of the details of what had happened that day because it might cause her to spiral down even worse.

"Okay. Ummm, ca . . . can I ask you something?" Ash said, even quieter than before.

"Sure," I said wondering what was coming.

"Have you guys been seeing Hunter?" she asked.

"Well, actually . . ." I looked at Spring for some help. "We have seen him around but we don't exactly know where he is. He has gone missing and we can't find him, remember? Why?" I said, keeping it simple.

"Oh gosh, he came to see me after you left yesterday. He seemed really scared and didn't want to talk about something but I couldn't figure out what," she said.

"He talked to you? He just stares at me and doesn't want to be seen by Spring, we can't figure out why," I said, keeping my voice calm even though my insides were screaming.

"Yeah, he was asking how I was doing and if I was okay, it seemed like he was really old for his age." She seemed to be gaining some more confidence in herself. "I mean, he wasn't acting like he was nine," she explained.

"Okay. If he comes back could you try to get him to tell you where he is or what happened to him because we are all really worried," I asked her, hoping it wasn't too big of a task for her.

"I can try, I can't promise anything," she said.

"Okay, thank you. Love you so much," I said and with that we left.

I couldn't help but think that it was weird that Hunter would talk to Ash but not to his own sister, but I didn't want to bring it up because I didn't want to seem like I was rubbing it in Spring's face. I thought that maybe it was because she was closer to his age or that she couldn't even totally remember what he said so she wouldn't be able to tell anyone a secret. On our way out of the hospital we ran into Alison. "Hey, Alison," I said.

"Hi, Al," said Spring.

"Hey, guys, y'all come to see Ash?" she asked.

"Yeah, and actually I was wondering if you saw a boy come to visit her," I asked, hoping to get some clue.

"Yeah actually, he came yesterday, said that he was your brother," she said turning to Spring.

"Yeah, he is. The thing is that he has gone missing," Spring said. "He left a note the other day saying that he didn't feel loved and that he had gone out to find himself, but he came back that day. Then, he went missing. He was out with his sister at the park and she came home but he didn't. We have been looking for him and we thought it was weird that he came to see Ash," she explained. "Did you hear anything that he said to her?" she asked.

"Oh my gosh! I am so sorry. I didn't realize he was missing, I would have tried to stop him if I had known. Do you have anything yet? We might be able to look at security footage and see if there is any sound," she suggested.

"Can you get us that kind of clearance?" I asked.

"Everybody knows you guys and if there is anything we can do to keep your family together then we will help. I think you can get in there yourself," she said with a smile on her face.

So off we went to find the security officer that would let us into to room with the footage. It wasn't long until we found one and really I could have gone into Ash's room if we couldn't find one.

"Hi, sir, we were wondering if we could look at some of the security footage from yesterday," Spring asked shyly.

"Why the hell would I give two teenagers access to that?" he said.

His reaction scared us because most of the policemen knew us and most were actually out looking for Hunter.

"Well, you see, sir, her brother has gone missing and my sister and a nurse said that he came here yesterday. The thing is, my sister won't say what he said to her and we were hoping to find that out to see where he is and find him," I explained. I had Spring be my sister so that it didn't cause any more tension than we needed in the moment.

"I am still not seeing why you think you can just walk up to me and ask for that clearance. I mean, you are just kids and you can't be walking around expecting to get everything you ask for. Where are your parents?" he questioned, he seemed to be getting madder and madder by the minute.

"We don't have any. Can I talk to another officer, please." Spring breezed over the question, hoping he wouldn't think about the answer.

"Sure, whatever," he replied. He called in an Officer James for us to talk to and walked away.

We waited a little bit before the new officer found us. He seemed to be nicer seeing as though he walked up to us smiling, rather than frowning. I relaxed a little and I felt Spring do the same next to me.

"Hi, girls. How is your search for Hunter going?" he asked. So he knew us, that is a good start.

"Actually, that is why we are here. My sister, you know, Ash, she said that he came to see her yesterday. And Alison, a nurse, said that she had seen him too. But, the thing is, my sister won't tell us what he said to her and we were hoping to be able to get into the security room to look at some footage and listen to some audio," I explained once more, in a little more depth than I had given the first officer.

"Oh, well, I can see what I can do. You most likely will have to have someone in there with you just to make sure you don't take anything, not that you will, but it'll be just a safety precaution," he said.

"That is fine, thank you. One more thing, what was up with the officer before you, the one that called you over here?" I asked, wanting to know if he was new or something.

"Oh, he lost some of his family and decided to go into policing. He just moved here yesterday and we thought it would be good to start him off with something easy. Why?" Officer James said.

"Well, he got really mad and said that us teenagers needed to stop thinking that we would get anything just because we asked for it. He definitely didn't recognize us so I thought that he was new," I said.

Officer James just smiled at us. "Yeah, he is probably just irritated that he was handed the hospital guard job on his first day here. I will talk to him and tell him about you guys' situation and try to get him to understand," he said.

"Thanks, we tried to tell him but he just wasn't listening," Spring said.

"All right. Well, I will take you to the room and I think someone will be in there, if you explain to them what you need there I bet they will let you in," he said.

"Thank you." And off he went. Spring and I gave each other looks and then decided to follow. On the way there I kept thinking about what Hunter could have said to Ash that was so bad or secretive that she couldn't even tell me. She tells me everything—from what she had for breakfast to the scary dream that she had that night. Or what Hunter could have wanted to tell Ash and not Spring, Ash isn't even related to him. I thought that maybe it was because they are close in age and maybe he was having issues like with his sense of mind and wanted help from someone his age. I was so caught up in thought that I hadn't realized that we had stopped and I ran into Spring.

"Oh, sorry. I was lost in thought. I will tell you later," I apologized.

"It's okay, we are here. Thanks for leading us to the right place Officer James, we most definitely would have gotten lost," Spring said.

When we got inside the room one of the officers looked up and then back down, like he knew what was happening, or he just decided to ignore us.

"Hi, officers. Um, we were hoping to be able to see some footage from last night because we think it might help us find her brother," I said. There were three of them, all doing different things and they all stopped to look at me.

"Hi, girls," said one of them, at least one of them knew us. "I can help you with that." But right as he was getting up, the officer that had been giving us trouble in the hallway got up and didn't look very happy.

"How the heck do you just let teenagers walk around and get everything they ask for? I mean, they are just kids," he said, still completely unaware of Spring and I's situation.

"Well, officer, I know you are new here. The girls raise their siblings on their own because they don't have their parents. So we are all pretty supportive of them and because one of the sibling's going missing, we are all on patrol to try to find him, if they say that they think that there is a way to find out some more information about where he is then we are going to go with it," the officer that greeted us said.

"But why not put them in foster care or with another family?" he asked.

"Alice here convinced us that she could take care of her sister so we let them stay together, and then when Spring's family died in a car crash we figured that if they lived close enough to each other they could be like co-parents and help each other out. They are very responsible girls and would do anything for their family," the officer kept explaining.

"I guess that makes sense. But I am still baffled by the whole thing," he said.

"Maybe if you didn't just judge us because we are teenagers, and I am not saying we aren't, you could think about how hard it would be to raise younger siblings by yourself." I snapped at him, kind of surprising myself. "You could think about how much we are freaking out because her brother is missing and my sister said that he came to see her.

Maybe you could help us find a missing person rather than sitting there questioning the police chief and the other members who have been here long before you and know our situation," I finished, proud of myself.

All of the other officers were kind of looking back in forth from me and the officers trying to figure out what is going to happen next. I looked at him and then I looked at Spring to try to figure out what we are going to do because I hadn't had expected to burst out like that, I didn't know how she was going to react.

"Well, I hope that we can find your brother," the officer said, motioning to Spring. "I didn't mean to seem disrespectful toward the other officers," he finished to the officer helping us.

After going through the footage, there was nothing, it just looked like Ash was talking to herself, we decided to go home and talk about what we had just figured out. We didn't know what to do with this information. Alison had said she had seen him and Ash said that he had talked to her, and the fact that he didn't show up on the security footage, everything was a little weird.

Spring decided that she and her sister would stay the night at my house seeing as though we needed to stay up and figure out a game plan, but when I got back I saw Callie's car outside of my house. When I walked in she was looking for something, I wanted to see what she was doing so Spring and I just stayed quiet for a little while. She was digging through the couches and had torn apart the kitchen already.

"Umm, Callie, what are you doing?" I said finally.

She jumped, clearly not knowing that we were there. "Oh, hi, girls. Nothing, I was just looking around," she said, kind of out of breath. But I could tell that she wasn't just looking around.

"No, you're not, Callie. What are you looking for? Are you sure you didn't have anything to do with Hunter missing?" I asked her, I knew that she didn't want to answer me for either question but I needed to know.

"Nothing, I swear," she replied a little too quickly. She was still lying.

"Okay, but I will tell you that the police have come and searched through the house, they might have taken whatever you were looking for," I said.

She went pale white. "What do you mean the police have been here?" she asked nervously.

"Exactly that. I told them about Hunter, which in turn caused me to tell them about you and you randomly leaving after we had asked you about Hunter the first time," I said, glad to see that I had scared her a little.

"Why would you do that, Alice? I thought you had said that you wouldn't say anything," she said, clearly getting mad.

"Well, when you had randomly left I thought that you had something to do with Hunter going missing, and when I told the chief what you did he wanted to search the house, so I let him. It's not like they haven't seen the house before, I wasn't nervous. I am just hoping that whatever they found can help us find Hunter, unless you want to tell us something," I explained to her. As I was talking she had to sit down. Obviously the police had found whatever she was looking for and apparently it was important.

"Come on, Spring, I think we should go the station and see what they found," I said turning to her, seeing her smiling at me.

Spring didn't like Callie, never has. She has seen me go through the entire hassle of getting the police to let me take care of my sister and then she went through it herself with her siblings. And now that Callie was back in our lives and Hunter has gone missing, everything was just in a bad situation.

When we had gotten to the station all of the officers greeted us.

"Hi, I was wondering if you have seen the officer who went through my house? Callie has come back and when we got home she was looking for something," I announced. I got dropped jaws to that. It was apparent that nobody but the one officer knew about Callie coming back and the fact that I had just announced it to everyone seemed to have shocked them.

"Hey, girls, I am right here," he said. "I think I might know what she was looking for, let me show you," he said leading us to the back where the interrogation rooms where. In one of the rooms the table was covered in things that they had gotten out of my house. A lot of them I recognized, while some I didn't.

"Now, can you tell me anything you don't recognize?" he said, and right away I told him. There was some of Ash's toys that I didn't have the guts to throw away because Dad had given them to her and I didn't want the day to come that she came home from the hospital and none of her stuff was there. However, one thing that really stuck out as unusual was a handkerchief, one that I had never seen before.

"The handkerchief looks weird. I have never seen it before and I am pretty sure that neither has Spring," I said looking at her.

"Yeah, I don't know anyone that carries a handkerchief," she said.

"Okay," said the officer. "I will make sure to look at that closely and then call you if we need anything else or if we find something," he finished.

"Okay," we said in unison, and then walked out of the room.

At home, Callie was still on the couch. It didn't look like she had moved at all while we were gone but I didn't trust her. Spring and I just walked in, looked at her, and then went up to my room.

In my room we started to think. "I don't know why Callie would have brought a handkerchief, if it is even hers," said Spring. "It's not like she is living in the past, she seems to be trying to catch up with your life."

"I know," I said. "I don't understand why she would take Hunter, if she did, she doesn't even know him. It's like she is trying to get back at me for Dad," I finished.

"I don't think she would do that, it wasn't your fault. I think that she hasn't changed and is still trying to jack with you and Ash's life," Spring said.

"Alice," I heard from downstairs. "Can you come down here?"

So, wondering what it was about, hoping it was her confessing to something, we both went downstairs. Much to our surprise, Hunter was with her.

"Don't try to talk to him," I whispered in Spring's ear. "I don't know what is happening and every time I have tried to talk to him he disappears," I said, warning her.

"What, Callie?" I said, a little annoyance in my voice that I didn't want there. "How did you find him?" I asked, now sounding worried.

"Well, I wanted to tell you that I didn't take him, he just walked in here wanting to talk to you. I also wanted to know if the police had taken my handkerchief, I have been looking for it," she said. Half of me wanted to believe her and the other half didn't trust her.

"Okay, well, yes, the police did take it and because neither one of us recognized it they are testing it for DNA. Obviously, they will find yours on it but if they find anyone else they will be suspicious. And I don't know if I should believe you about Hunter," I said. Taking a deep breath I turned to Hunter. "Hi, Hunter," I said.

"Hi," he said. "I wanted to see if you could help me. But I don't want to worry Spring because I am okay, just not at the house," he said, not even looking at Spring. It's like he couldn't see her.

"Okay," I said. "I will make sure that she won't get worried about you. What do you want me to know, how can I help you?" I asked.

"Umm, well, I am still in town, I don't know where exactly because I haven't really been outside. I don't know who took me, if they are a boy, or a boy acting like a girl. That is pretty much all I know," he finished.

"Okay," I said. "Is there a way that we can get to you? I want to try to help you. And I don't know if I should believe Callie. Do you know if she has anything to do with this?" I asked.

"Umm, I don't think so, I haven't heard her voice before. But I can understand why you don't trust her because of everything she has done to your family. But I am pretty sure that she didn't take me," he said, sounding old.

I turned to Spring to see what she thought about this, but she was just staring at Hunter, trying not to cry. She knew that he didn't want her there and that was hurting her feelings.

"So, can I ask why you haven't shown up at your own house? I mean, I have no idea how you are even talking to us, but I know that she really is worried about you. And if you can answer, why did you go talk to Ash? She isn't related to you," I questioned.

"I haven't gone home because I am afraid to honestly. I think that Spring will be mad at me because I couldn't do anything about it or I haven't come home. And I got to talk to Ash because she doesn't know who I am and is willing to talk to me. It seems like it is easier to talk to her than my actual family. I am talking to you by a video recorder that I hacked, the people don't actually know I have had contact with you guys," he finished.

"Okay, I am sure Spring won't be disappointed in you, she would really like to see you. And I think that you shouldn't go see Ash just because she doesn't recognize you doesn't mean it is okay to talk to her. You are essentially unloading onto her something that she doesn't need to know but I am glad that you are talking to someone. If you get caught talking to us, who knows what they will do to you, just make sure you are careful. I hope we can find a way to get you home soon," I said, warning him.

"I will, thank you," he said, and with that he disappeared. I guess that is what happened when I had turned around in the kitchen and he was gone.

I turned to Spring. "I think that he might be coming around soon, it seemed like he got the message that you were just worried about him. And I think that he wouldn't be able to video chat if he were in serious trouble," I said, trying to calm her nerves. I saw that it didn't work.

"I don't know what to do now. I mean, like you said, it seems like he is okay but I can't help being worried and scared. What if I don't get my brother back? What if he is in more trouble than he says he is? What if he is being forced to say all that stuff so that we don't look for him or we are looking in the wrong direction?" Spring was getting worked up. I didn't know how to help her, there is really nothing I can do for her now that she has heard from her brother that he is okay.

I don't know what to do. It has been a couple of days and everything has gone awry. Hunter has gone missing and Callie is back. We think that Callie has something to do with him going missing but we aren't exactly sure. Hunter came through a video today and was talking about how he was okay and in the city, he also said that he doesn't know exactly where he is or exactly who took him. I don't know what to do.

I needed to get this off my chest, but writing it down didn't seem to help. As I wrote it made me realize that I really didn't know what to do, how to help the people I love.

When I came out of my room Spring had gone home to make sure her sister was okay and Callie was still sitting on the couch, looking dumbfounded.

"Why do you still think that I have something to do with Hunter going missing?" she asked me seeming hurt, like she felt betrayed.

"Well, the day that you show up is the day that Spring tells me Hunter has gone missing. We had gone to the hospital and the police station and when we got back you were looking for something, we figured that you looked suspicious. And then when we went back to the station, there was a handkerchief that neither Spring nor I recognized, we thought it was yours," I explained. I saw that she didn't know what to say because she just stared ahead and looked at a wall.

"But, why would you automatically think it was mine?" she asked.

"I mean, we had never seen it before, no one we know carries a handkerchief, and you were the only new person in my life. I didn't know who else to blame it on. I know that the officers who came and looked through the house can't have one because it isn't part of their uniforms," I said. "All signs sort of pointed to you."

"But why?" she continued to ask.

"I don't know what to tell you, Callie. You just try to walk back into my life and act like nothing has changed, but everything has changed. Dad's gone, Ash is in the hospital, and my girlfriend's brother is missing. You want to act like nothing has happened. You think that I can just forgive you after you left us for five years, but guess what? You made all of these bad things happen to my family, you caused Dad to kill himself. And when a boy, close enough to be my brother, goes missing, yeah, I am going to blame you because I don't trust you! I don't even know whether I can let you stay in this house because I don't know what you are going to do! And I am sorry if me not trusting you is somehow hurting your feelings, but what if the roles were swapped, what if you were me, would you trust you?" I finished, almost crying. I was done with the acting like I was okay with everything, Spring wasn't here so I didn't have to be the tough one while her brother didn't even want to talk to her, and I don't have to protect Ash because she is in the hospital.

Callie opened her arms, like she wanted to hug me, like a normal mother would do when their child is crying, but I had just finished telling her that I didn't trust her. How could she expect me to collapse into her arms?

"I don't understand you, Callie. I tell you that I don't trust you, I blame you for everything that has happened, and yet you want a hug," I said to her turning around and sitting in the chair behind me. "What makes you think that I would want to hug you right now? I don't care if you are my mom and are supposed to do these things. I am going to Spring's house to make sure she is okay," I finished, turning away and walking out the door.

At Spring's house, the atmosphere isn't any better. She is worried about her brother, as she should be, but I can tell that there is something else on her mind.

"Hey, are you okay?" I asked.

"I mean, it was nice to hear Hunter say that he was okay but I keep on thinking that there is another layer to it. Whatever it is," she said.

"I know. I hate that I can't help you or him. I don't know what to do either," I said, giving up on trying to convince her that everything was okay. Because honestly, I felt the same way.

"I know you were trying to cheer me up, and I am sorry that I am in such a bad mood. I just don't know what else to think about except for the fact that my brother, whom I was put in charge of, was kidnapped and now I don't know where he is," Spring said, getting everything off her chest.

"I know mostly how you feel. I felt the same way when Ash got in her big fight and ended up in the hospital, but I don't know how to help you since I don't know how to relate to the feeling of your brother missing. I hope that we find him or get any hints as to where he is soon," I said honestly.

"Thanks for coming over and checking on me, I think that I would really want to be alone and play with my sister. I am sorry about Callie not able to be trusted and not knowing what to do about her," Spring said. I understood what she needed, so I left her. I was glad that she had another sibling to think about and that she is the kind of person that won't forget about everyone else because of something going awry. I think that she also is glad to have a distraction, to help her not worry about Hunter all the time.

Back at home Callie was still sitting on the couch. I still didn't know what to do with her. I know that I hurt her by saying all of those things but I didn't know what else to say to her, she had been getting on my nerves.

"Callie," I said tenderly. "I am sorry about all of those things I said. I just don't know what to do about everything and I freaked out. But I also want you to know that pretty much all of the things I said is what I feel. I want you to know that I don't consider you to be my mom. I am sorry if that hurts you but you missed all of the growing up that you should have been here for," I said, starting to cry as all of my feelings came out, "because you left, I had to pick up the pieces of Dad dying and then Ash ending up in the hospital. Because you left, I have to take care of everything that a mom should and I had to drop out of school. I could be in a way better place right now if you hadn't had just given up. That is what it was, it was you just giving up because you thought that we didn't like you, but guess what, you were supposed to be our mom, you were supposed to be the one to never give up and to be a role model to Ash and I." This time I was crying. I realized then that I did want her to be there for me but I also knew that I wouldn't be able to connect with her the way that I wanted to, the way a mother and daughter should. "I do want you to be back in our life, but how do I know that you won't just up and leave again. I can't do that to Ash again. You can't do that to both of us again," I finished.

When I was able to see again, Callie was also crying. I know that she understood now. "I know, and I don't know what I am going to do. I want you to know that, me leaving wasn't me giving up. I didn't know what else to do."

"So, you did give up," I said, interrupting her. "You didn't want to try to make everything better."

"I mean, I did, I just didn't know how. I am sorry that your dad killed himself, shouldn't you be mad at him too? I mean, he left you as much as I did," she said.

"I already did that, it just brought me back to being upset with you. I understood why he did it, it wasn't the right thing to do, but I understand. He thought that you had left because you didn't love him," I said.

"I realize that you have already gone through the emotions for your dad. And I understand that he thought it was my fault, and I know that I shouldn't have left you guys high and dry but, like I said, I didn't know what to do," Callie said. "I left because I thought your father didn't love me. I know that is a lame excuse but it is the truth. I didn't know what else to tell you."

"Well, you can promise me that you will stay and help me, stay and support Ash, just stay," I said, taking a deep breath to collect my thoughts. "You can promise me that you have nothing to do with Hunter going missing. You can promise me that you are trustworthy and that I have nothing to worry about," I said.

"Well, I honestly don't know if I am staying. I don't know what I am going to do. I can promise you that I had nothing to do with Hunter and that I am trustworthy," Callie said.

"If you don't know if you are going to stay, which I don't even know why it is a question in your mind, then how do I know that I can trust you?" I said.

"It's a question in my mind because I don't know if I would be ready to take care of Ashley and you, it is a lot of responsibility to jump right into," she said.

"It wouldn't be a lot of responsibility if you hadn't had left. I don't know why you are complaining so much, it is all your fault," I said, getting mad again. I mean, it really was.

"Now, Alice, you don't need to get mad, I already know that you are angry at me," Callie said, trying to act like a mom.

"No, I do! You don't get to reprimand me anymore, I have grown up faster than I should have and it is your fault. Right now I should be in school, Ash should be in school, Dad should be alive, you should be my mom," I said, now really angry.

Interrupting us was a knock at my door, and I am glad something did distract us because who knows where that was going. When I opened the door it was the police chief.

"Hi, Chase," I said kindly, giving him a hug. "Come on in." So he did. I could tell he had at least some news, good or bad I didn't know. "This is Callie, my mother," I said introducing him.

"So you're the person who put this family in this mess," the officer said. I did not expect him to say anything.

"I have come to the realization," Callie replied, she seemed a little ashamed. "And who might I be talking to?" she questioned.

"I am Officer Adams, the Chief Officer at the city police station. You better be lucky that I like my job because if not, well, I don't know if I would be containing myself right now. Do you have any idea what you put these girls through?" Officer Adams said.

"I have been informed, yes," Callie replied a little too calm, a little too suspicious. I could see Officer Adams's wheels turning, analyzing Callie's response.

"Do you know the bullying that they both have gone through? The torment Ash has gone through? Do you know that only Alice is allowed to see her because 'friends' would come into the hospital and make fun of her?" Officer Adams questioned her.

"Officer, I just got done ranting to her, actually you interrupted. I have a feeling you came here to tell me something, I am hoping it is something about Hunter and what we can do to get him back," I said after noticing that Callie was getting overwhelmed.

"Okay," he said to me, then turning back to Callie he said, "be prepared to be put under the hot lamp."

I led Officer Adams into the kitchen. "So, you came here to tell me something before we got distracted with Callie. What is it? Anything about Hunter? I have some new information to give you," I said rushing.

"Okay, we did a fingerprint scan on the handkerchief to see if we could find anything. A person named Claire came up. What was weird is that we couldn't find a last name for her. She lives in the city just next to us called Baycliff. Her house is about twenty miles from Pineridge, where we are. If you want we can go to her house and see why her things were in your house," he suggested.

"Here's what I think, I don't know why any of this Claire girl's stuff is in my house, but I don't think it was her who took Hunter. He was at Spring's house when he was taken, or that is what he told us. I will have to think about going to see Claire," I said. After I finished I heard a cough from the other room, I knew Callie was listening in. "I also don't think that Callie had anything to do with Hunter. He came to talk to me again," I said.

"What, when? What did he say?" Officer Adams asked excitedly.

"Well, he told me that he didn't want to talk to Spring because he thought that she would be disappointed. He also said that he didn't know where he was or who took him." I started to recall what Hunter had said to us earlier.

"Well that leads us nowhere," Officer Adams sighed after I had finished.

"I know. And we can't even trace a signal because he has access to some sort of holographic technology. I don't even know if we have been talking to the current Hunter. It could be a weird recording that can only answer certain questions like in movies," I said, just having that realization. "I think that I should go get Spring if we are going to talk about Hunter."

"I think that is a good idea," he said. With that, I left to go to Spring's house.

When I walked in, I found Spring sitting in the kitchen just staring blankly ahead of her. She looked worse than when I had last seen her.

"Hey, love. I want you to come to my house. Officer Adams is there with some information, and I want you and your sister to come over for a while. I think you need to get out of your house," I said calmly.

"Okay, let me go get her and pack up some stuff," Spring said softly. When we got back to my house, Officer Adams was talking to Callie.

"Hi, Spring," he said when he noticed us walking in. "How are you doing?"

"I'm okay I guess. It's a lot for me to handle on my own right now," Spring replied. "I hear you have some new information for me." So, the three of us went to the kitchen, Spring's sister went to play with her toys, and Callie just sat on the couch.

Officer Adams told Spring everything he had told me while I made sure she wasn't going to freak out too much.

"Of course I want to go see this Claire chick. I want to know why she might be a lead and if she has any idea where Hunter might be," she said, getting anxious.

"Okay, we should set a day so that you can find someone to watch your sister and so I can figure out what we are going to do with Callie," he said.

"Yeah, what are you going to do with her?" I asked.

"I don't know. My first instinct is to take her to the station for questioning but I know that she will not be comfortable there with how many people support you and Spring. But I want to question her on why she left. I don't know," he said.

"You probably won't get anything from her on why she left other than she thought that Dad didn't love her. But you do whatever you want with her, I don't care," I said.

"Okay. I say that we meet back here tomorrow afternoon, after you have settled in," he said to Spring. "And hopefully we will have some sort of plan."

The next day, Spring had called one of her sister's friends and got it arranged for her to stay with them for a couple of days. I still didn't know what Officer Adams was going to do with Callie. I thought that he was going to take her in, if he didn't I was going to have her stay in a hotel because I didn't trust her in the house by herself.

"Hi, girls." I heard around 3:00 later that day, knowing it was Officer Adams.

"In here, Officer," I called to him.

"Okay, here is what I have," he started. "I hope you are doing okay, Spring. I think I am going to take Callie in and have someone other than me question her. I also think that we should go to Claire's house. We should leave, maybe tomorrow after lunch to get there before dinner."

"That'll work for us, I think," Spring said. After that, Officer Adams left with Callie and Spring and I got ready to leave the next day. As we were getting ready my nerve level went up. I was glad that we had a police officer going with us because I wouldn't know what to do or say.

Officer Adams showed up the next day at 1:30 so that we could leave. "You guys ready?" he asked us. He could probably tell that we were both really nervous.

"As we will ever be," I said and off we went.

The car ride was silent, none of us wanted to talk because we were so nervous about what we might find.

"What are we going to say?" Spring asked, breaking the silence.

"I think I am going to start with seeing if she recognized the handkerchief and go from there," Officer Adams said.

"What if she doesn't?" I asked.

"I guess we will go home and find another lead. Maybe Callie will give us something," he answered.

"In a strange way I hope she has some sort of connection with this because then we can continue instead of having to start over," Spring said.

"I can understand that," said Officer Adams.

"I don't know. I feel like I don't want it to be her but I think that my brain wants something to blame Callie on," I said.

"But don't you want it to be something other than my brother going missing?" Spring asked me.

"I guess that is true. I hope that the officer questioning her finds something against her," I said, sounding kind of evil.

"Now, Alice," Officer Adams started, "don't you want her to stay in your life?"

"Not really, I mean, I have survived this long without her. She has already lost the privilege of being my mother, you both should know this," I said.

"I know, Alice, but at least you have a parent that could possibly be in your life," Spring said.

"It would almost be better if she were dead. I know that is terrible to say but it is the way I feel. If she were dead then I feel like I could have some closure instead of having to deal with her now. And if she had been like your parents, Spring, then she wouldn't have left and maybe Dad would still be alive. My life is like this because she just packed up and left," I said. In the middle of me ranting about Callie we had stopped in front of Claire's house. "Let's just go in. I don't want to talk about this anymore."

Officer Adams knocked on the door with his badge ready. The door opened and a woman answered.

"Are you Claire?" Officer Adams said.

"Yes," she replied. "Who are you?"

"I am Officer Adams of Pineridge City and this is Alice and Spring. We have some questions for you if you will answer them for us," he said.

"Um, okay. Come on in." Claire invited us into her house and led us into the living room.

"So, we found something that we believe belongs to you in Alice's house. Do you recognize this?" he asked, pulling out the handkerchief in a plastic bag.

"Yeah, my grandma had one of those and then she gave it to my mom, but I haven't seen her use it in forever," Claire answered honestly.

"Why, then, did we find fingerprints on it? And why was it in Alice's house?" he asked her.

"My mom left a couple of days ago since she has been living with me. I am not sure where she went. She could have gone to your house. I don't know," she said.

"My mom just showed up at my house a couple of days ago," I said to her. I hope that Callie isn't her mom, too, there is no way she could be, I mean, Callie is too young to have another kid anyways.

"What is your mom's name?" asked Spring. We gave each other the same look after she asked that question and I knew she was thinking the same thing I was.

"Callie," she answered simply.

"No, no, no. There is no way that my Callie could possibly be someone else's mom," I said. We had left the house to do some thinking and we were all in Spring and I's hotel room. "I mean, right. She is too young, right?" I said, looking at both of them.

"Has Callie ever told you anything about having other kids?" Officer Adams asked me.

"No! How could this be possible?" I asked.

"She could have gotten pregnant before she met your father and had the kid, she could have had a child with him before they got married and not told him. But if any of those things are true, most moms who are hiding a kid wouldn't stay in contact with the kid," he said, giving some explanations.

"I know, do you think she will tell the officer questioning her? I mean, she didn't even tell me. Maybe that is what they were fighting over when she left. Can you tell your staff to ask her about that?" I said, going through a million thoughts at once.

"Yeah, I just got to call them," he said and stepped outside into the hallway.

"What are you going to do if they do find out that Claire and Callie are related? We still don't know if she had anything to do with Hunter," Spring said to me.

"I think we have to go back and ask her some more questions. See if she knows anything. I don't know what I am going to do if they are related because then that means that I am related to her and I don't want to be related to the person that is possibly affiliated with the people that took your brother," I said. "I also don't want to think about my mother having a child when she was sixteen or having a kid with Dad and not telling him, what kind of person would do that, how would you hide a pregnancy for nine months?" I said, mainly thinking out loud now.

"I don't know, Alice, I don't know," Spring said.

Officer Adams walked back into the room. "So I told my team to ask her about a possible other child," he said.

"Okay," I said. "Spring and I decided that we want to go back to Claire's house and ask her about Hunter since we didn't get to do that before. But I think we should go tomorrow so that we have some time to think about what happened today and possibly get some answers from home."

"That is a good idea," he agreed.

Back at Claire's house we told her about our Callie and how we think that they are the same person.

"Why would she hide us from each other?" Claire had the same question I did.

"When did she come into your life? Because she just walked back into mine," I asked her, really wanting it not to be my mom.

"About five years ago, I was living with my godparents and they had told me that she had died in a freak accident. I was really surprised when she showed up," she explained.

"She and my dad had a fight about five years ago and she walked out of my life, I am assuming that she came to you. I think that you were her escape from my family. Do you have her phone number?" I asked. I didn't have a number for Callie but if she does and my Callie answers then it is true and the police don't have to investigate that.

"I do but when I tried to call her recently it said that the number had been disconnected. I wasn't worried about it though because her phone does that sometimes," she said.

"Do you think that you could call her later today and if I give you my phone number could you call me and update me?" I asked.

"Sure," she said and we swapped numbers.

"We have one more thing to ask you about," Officer Adams said, "we were wondering if you knew about a boy named Hunter. He is Spring's little brother and he has gone missing, we thought that maybe you might have some information for us or if you knew if Callie had anything to do with him going missing."

"I don't recognize the name, I am sorry," she said to Spring. "I will say that my mom kept some journals that she never let me see, maybe they might give you some information," she turned to Officer Adams.

"Can you bring them to us or us to them, please." We followed her up the stairs and into what looked like the master bedroom.

She reached under the bed and pulled out about three journals that looked full to the breaking point.

"This is insane!" I said, realizing the extent of Callie's craziness. While we went through the notebooks it became apparent that the two Callies were the same person, she kept talking about me and Ash. She also had pictures of us growing up, of Ash at school, of the river they found Dad at. "So she knew that Dad killed himself, she knew why Ash was in the hospital, she straight up lied to my face. What the heck?" I said, getting mad at her once again.

"It looks like it. She never mentioned another family to me," Claire said. "What is going on here?" she finally sounded a little surprised.

"Why is it just now that you sounded surprised?" Officer Adams asked. "It seems a little weird that you don't seem to think that any of this is out of the blue." Claire just sat there, not talking.

"Well?" I asked her.

"I kind of knew where she was going and she had told me that she was going to see some family but I didn't know that we would be related or that she had had another kid, or that she had left a family for five years," she explained.

"I think that you should try to call her and ask her about us. We will stay here and I would like you to have the phone in speaker so that if she lies we can tell you," Officer Adams told her.

"I don't know if she will answer, I tried to call her last night and she didn't answer. It didn't say that her number was inactive but she didn't answer," Claire said. I think she was trying to get us to believe that she couldn't get in contact with her.

"I don't think you called her last night," Officer Adams said.

"Me too, I know when someone is lying, now that I have had become a mom. You, my dear, are lying," I said. I wanted to get her to stop protecting Callie, I mean, if she would have known what Callie was doing to my family I am sure that she wouldn't be helping her right now.

"Okay, what if I didn't call her, why does that matter to you? I mean, it's not like she is doing anything to you guys. Why do you want to know so much?" Claire was getting angry with us, kind of defensive.

"Well, if you knew what I have gone through and what my sister has gone through then you would understand," I started.

"And she might possibly have something to do with my brother going missing. I just want to check everything because Callie came back the same day that Hunter went missing, that can't be a coincidence," Spring said, surprising me with standing up for our side of the argument. Spring was a person that normally doesn't speak up in these sort of situations, preferring to listen and gather information that way.

"But, why do you guys keep coming here?" Claire kept asking us questions.

"You are our only tie to Callie and our only way of getting any information about her without actually asking her," Officer Adams answered for us. He seemed to notice that she stopped willingly complying with everything we asked of her. "Are you sure that you haven't heard of a Hunter or the fact that a kid named Hunter has gone missing?" he asked her again.

"Mom told me that she was going to see some family, I assumed it was just relatives that I didn't know about or friends that she didn't want to introduce me to. She might have said Hunter but I don't know, I wasn't really paying attention to what she was telling me," she told us.

"Okay," I said. We kept going through the journals, not finding anything else about my family or about Callie keeping in contact with Dad or the fact that she even had more kids.

"I found something!" Spring said.

"Finally, what is it?" I said scooting closer to her.

"It says *I think that I should go see Alice and Ash and their father. I know that it has been a while and I don't know how they are going to react.* That is dated back two years ago. She has been thinking about you guys for a while before she even got the guts to come back. But on the next page, a couple of days later she talks about me, she says, *I know that Alice has either a really close friend or a girlfriend, I don't know which yet. I want to be in their life but I don't know what I would do.* So she doesn't know here that your dad actually died," Spring said, turning to me.

"So, she has pictures of where they found him but she didn't know that he had killed himself. That seems a little weird. I feel like she is trying to cover something up if someone were to read these books," I said slowly. "What if she started to see Hunter when she noticed you, I mean your entire family was over all the time, I am sure that if she had someone spying on us she would have seen him. Did you find anything about him in here?" I asked her going through the pages again

"Not yet, but I haven't gotten through the entire book yet. I will look, this is insane," she said.

"I found a picture of him," Officer Adams said.

"What?" Spring and I said at the same time. He showed us a picture of Hunter and Molly at the park while Spring and I were in the background getting ice cream for everyone.

"I think that we should go home. I have some bones to pick with Callie and I am not going to accept lies this time. Not now that I know the truth, or most of it," I said to him. I was done finding all of this stuff. I needed some real answers from Callie. After packing up and eating some lunch, we headed home.

At home, I had Officer Adams bring Callie to my house to try to get some answers from her. Spring showed up with Molly a couple of minutes later and sent her upstairs to play with toys.

"So, Callie. While we were away we met someone and found some interesting things about you," I said, my voice shaky with anticipation of what I might find out. "I wanted to ask you some questions."

"Okay, go ahead." She sounded confident that what we had found wasn't going to reveal anything.

"Who is Claire? And why are there a bunch of journals at her house? Why do you have pictures of Spring's life and mine? What else have you lied to us about?" I said, bombarding her with questions.

She took a deep breath. "So you met Claire," she said.

"Yes, her fingerprint was on a handkerchief that we found in the house after you had left in a hurry," Officer Adams said.

"So you found my handkerchief," she said in the same tone.

"Yes, after you left and we did a search, it was the only thing that we found that was out of the ordinary," he explained to her in a way that made it sound like she was a little kid.

"You know, we already told you all of this. Are you going to actually answer any of my questions?" I asked, getting annoyed with her darting around everything.

"Okay, so since you met Claire you already know that she is my daughter. I kept journals there because I needed to write down what was happening so that I didn't have it all bottled up. I would come down to visit you guys and then chicken out so I just took pictures of you so I still knew what you looked like as you were growing up and Spring just happened to be there," she said, explaining everything.

"But why did you have pictures of the place that they found Dad? Did you know that he had killed himself?" I said, my voice getting louder.

"That was our favorite spot to go when we were dating and I wanted a picture of it. I didn't realize that that is where your father went," she said.

"You seem really calm about the fact that we pretty much just went through your other life. What is going on?" Officer Adams said.

"When I told Claire that I was going to see some family, she didn't question me. I decided to bring the handkerchief to plant it."

"You wanted us to meet her?" I asked, bewildered.

"Yes, because I knew that if I kept that secret for any longer it would come out one way or another I figured that it would be best for you to meet her on your terms with everything that has happened to you," she said.

"Do you realize that we went to her house thinking that it was her that took Hunter or had something to do with Hunter? I think Officer Adams was ready to arrest her if he thought she might be a suspect," I said to her. "We then thought that we might find out something about Hunter in your journals but we just found creepy pictures of me and Spring."

"I know, I am sorry. I don't know what else to tell you." She was starting to sound angry.

"Did you lie to me about anything else? Because I am back to strongly thinking that you had something to do with Hunter going missing. I mean, I told you about my dream, right?" I asked her.

"You didn't tell me about a dream," she said, leaning forward.

"I dreamt that you had come to my door in the middle of the night and told me that you had taken Hunter by 'accident,'" I told her.

"I did!" she told me covering her mouth immediately after. She hadn't meant to say that.

"What!" Spring and I yelled at the same time. "Why?" I asked her.

"I am being honest. I didn't mean to take him," she said.

"That is still not a proper explanation," Spring said.

"You have to tell us the entire story," I told her. "We need the whole thing, no details left out, no going off on side roads about why you know these things," I said to her, still mad and trying not to yell anymore since Molly was upstairs and I am sure could hear us.

"Okay, here you go. Before I got to your house the other day I saw him and Molly playing at the park, I was assuming that you were close because I thought Spring was close. So when I didn't see you, I asked Hunter. He told me that you were at your house and Spring was at hers. When I asked him where that was he wouldn't tell me. He thought that I already knew because everyone in this town knows you guys and he went back to playing with Molly. I guess he thought that I had left to find you and thought that my car was Spring's car and got in. When I heard the doors open and close, it scared me because I wasn't paying attention. I was trying to figure out what I was going to tell you and Ashley. So, anyway, when I heard the doors, I jumped and hit the gas causing us to move. So, he got out and ran, Molly just got out and walked home. I thought that he had ran home because they went the same direction. So when you guys said that he went missing I was shocked. I left in a hurry that day because I went to look for him and the handkerchief is my lucky thing. I found him in an abandoned house and set up a camera for him to talk to you guys with. I brought him food and water and wore a costume so he wouldn't know it was me 'helping him.' I don't know why he was in the house or how he got there I just know he was there. I didn't know what to do, and then you kept asking me about it and I didn't know what to say. If I had told the truth you would have been mad at me, so I lied," Callie said, finishing her story.

"So you thought that not telling us was going to make it better?" I asked her, surprised. "And you thought that helping him in a different way than bringing him home was a good idea?"

"I didn't know what to do, I didn't expect you guys to be in the situation that you are in. And I didn't know if the people that took him was going to be back to look for him," she said, still trying to redeem herself.

"That doesn't make any of this better, you better be ready to take us all to this abandoned house," Spring told her.

"I will take you now if you want to go," she said.

"You better. Officer Adams, will you look after Molly while we are gone?" Spring asked him.

"Sure."

After about thirty minutes in the car, we pulled up to the house. I realized that there was no way that Hunter could have walked all the way there by himself, it would have taken him four hours. It made me start to question the truth in Callie's story.

I didn't know what to expect when we walked in, but it looked like it had been demoed because there were no walls and floors were straight wood.

We saw Hunter in the middle with a table and a camera set up on it. Spring went running toward him and when he heard her he opened his mouth as if he was expecting food.

"No, Hunter, it's me. I have come to take you home," Spring said to him. He smiled. "Can you talk, Hunter?" she asked him, he just shook his head in reply. "Okay, just hang on a minute." After a while she got him out of the chair that he was tied up in and we started to leave.

Callie stood in front of the door and said, "I am sorry, Alice, I don't know if I can let you do this. I don't want to disappoint Claire."

"What do you mean, you brought us all this way and now you are saying that we can't take him? What has happened to you?" I asked her.

"Claire sent me to get him because she believes that he could do some danger to this area. We said the whole relative thing to keep our stories straight. I don't know the whole reason why she thought that but she did and I am her partner in it, as well as her mom," she said.

"Well, we are getting through and you can't stop us, I want this fiasco to be over and when it is, I want you out of our lives," I told her. "I don't know why you thought any of this was a good idea, but I am just letting you know that it wasn't."

"I mean, why did you lie to us about Hunter! It just makes you look even more crazy than you already are," Spring said, holding Hunter close to her side.

Getting through her was harder than I expected, after being yelled at I thought that she might just have given up seeing as though that is what she had done in the past. She and I had a tussle and I ended up having to knock her down to actually get by her. I took her car so that she was really stuck there unless she decided to walk home, and that likely wasn't going to happen. When we got in the car Hunter took a deep breath.

"Hunter, what happened?" Spring tried talking to him again.

"I don't know," he said, his voice raspy from not being able to talk. He started to curl into Spring's lap. "I was running home, away from Callie, and someone took me to that house. I was being fed and given water but I don't, well I didn't, know who was doing all of it. I am glad to be out of there," he said, sighing again, I could tell he was tired and that he needed to be with his sister.

"I am glad you are safe and we are going to keep an eye on you to make sure they don't come back," I said to him.

"Thank you, guys," he said, falling asleep fully curled up in Spring's lap.

At home we found Officer Adams playing with Molly and when she saw her brother, she was super happy.

"Molly, I think that Hunter just wants to rest right now," I said to her, hurt to see the disappointed look on her face.

"Girls, I want to know everything that happened," Officer Adams said. We recalled everything for him so that he knew it all.

"I want you to keep someone either in your team or from the other team close to Callie and Claire because they are lunatics," I added at the end.

"Agreed, I will have someone put on that," he said.

"I think we are okay for now, Chase, thank you. I am glad we found Hunter and I told Callie to stay out of our lives, I was better off without her," I said to him. "Now, I am going to see Ash and update her on everything that has happened."

"Thank you for helping me, guys," Spring said to both of us. "I am going to take Hunter and Molly home and get everything settled, thank you again."

"No problem, Spring, it is what I am here for. I want to keep officers at both of your houses, or at least around them so that if Callie or Claire do come back you have someone protecting you," he said to us.

"Okay, thank you, Officer Adams," I said and we went our separate ways.

At the hospital I found Callie sitting and talking to Ash. "What are you doing here?" I yelled and ran toward her.